BLAST TO THE PAST

#5

Sacagawea's Strength

By Stacia Deutsch and
Rhody Cohon
Illustrated by David Wenzel

Aladdin Paperbacks
New York   London   Toronto   Sydney

To SMC, All my love, RYC

ALADDIN PAPERBACKS
An imprint of Simon & Schuster Children's Publishing Division
1230 Avenue of the Americas, New York, NY 10020
Text copyright © 2006 by Stacia Deutsch and Rhody Cohon
Illustrations copyright © 2006 by David Wenzel
All rights reserved, including the right of reproduction
in whole or in part in any form.
ALADDIN PAPERBACKS and colophon are registered
trademarks of Simon & Schuster, Inc.
Designed by Lisa Vega.
The text of this book was set in Minion.
The illustrations are rendered in Winsor Newton watercolor.
Manufactured in the United States of America
First Aladdin Paperbacks edition June 2006
2 4 6 8 10 9 7 5 3 1
The Library of Congress Control Number 2005930112
ISBN-13: 978-1-4169-1270-5
ISBN-10: 1-4169-1270-3

Contents

Bored

"Did you hear that?" I looked around anxiously. "I swear I just heard a bear growl."

"What are you taking about, Abigail?" Zack asked me, making a crazy sign with his finger around his ear. He turned to his twin brother. "Did you hear anything, Jacob?"

"I don't think so," Jacob replied, cupping his ear to hear better. "Nope. Nothing."

"I wish Abigail really did hear a bear," Zack said with a yawn. I could see his tonsils. "We could use some excitement. I'm bored," he moaned, stretching his arms and yawning again.

"Me too," Jacob added, sighing. "This isn't how I wanted to spend the afternoon."

Usually, I love Mr. Caruthers's assignments. Jacob and Zack are always excited by social studies too. But today's project was cartography. And as far as I could tell, there was nothing more dull in the entire universe.

Mr. C had explained that cartography is the art of making maps. We were supposed to draw in a journal an accurate map of the shallow creek bed that runs behind our school. He told us to pay special attention to the direction of the creek and which way the water flowed.

Next to the map, we had to describe any plants and animals we saw. Mr. C even said we needed to sketch little pictures of the bugs we found.

This was definitely the most horrible project in the whole history of social studies.

There were four of us in our cartography group: Jacob, Zack, Bo, and me. Only Bo was interested in the class project. He was standing near a bush and holding the long iron chain Mr. C had given us. "Abigail," he called, "would you mind holding one end of this chain against that rock over there?"

Mr. C had told us the iron chain was called a two-pole chain. A "pole" is a unit of measurement equal to sixteen and a half feet. Each link was 7.92 inches. The whole chain was thirty-three feet long. Bo liked using the two-pole chain. By counting the links, he could figure out exactly how far it was from the bush to the rock and then put them both on our map.

I didn't really want to, but I went to help Bo anyway. "It could be worse," I remarked to Jacob and Zack. Looking over my shoulder, I glanced over at the rest of our social studies classmates wandering around the creek bed. "Eliana Feinerman's group didn't even get a chain to measure stuff. They have two sticks and a bunch of rocks."

"Yeah," Jacob replied. "And Shanika Washington's group has it real bad too. They have to make a new map by copying and correcting an old one from the school library."

I picked up the end of the chain and placed it against the rock. Bo dragged the other end to the bush. "Well," I commented, watching Bo stretch the chain tight, "at least Bo's having fun."

Zack looked at Bo and joked, "Yeah, well, Roberto Rodriquez is new to our school. He probably doesn't know how to have fun." Because he was joking, Zack winked when he used Bo's full, real name.

Bo laughed softly and kept counting.

After another huge yawn, Zack opened our journal book and wrote in big letters: HISTORY CLUB? Zack turned the book toward me so I could see.

"No clue," I replied with a frown and a shrug.

Usually after school on Mondays, Bo, Jacob, Zack, and I have a History Club meeting. During History Club, our cool social studies teacher, Mr. Caruthers, sends us on a time-travel mission to visit someone famous in American history.

Mr. C invented a time-travel computer. The computer looks like a hand-held video game with four red buttons and a large screen. Slipping a cartridge into the back takes us to the past. Pulling out the cartridge brings us home again.

Our teacher told us that American history is in danger. He showed us a little black book full of names. For some mysterious reason, all the famous

Americans in Mr. C's book were quitting. They weren't inventing, or speaking out, or fighting for what was right. They were giving up their dreams!

Mr. C wanted more time to focus on his newest invention, so he asked the four of us to time-travel for him. He needed us to save history from changing forever!

So far, we'd been very successful in all of our adventures. We'd managed to keep history on track. It was amazing since the computer only gave us two hours to get the job done.

We're so good at time travel, Jacob, Zack, Bo, and I totally thought that we'd be hopping through time today on another History Club adventure. It was Monday, after all. But late last week, Mr. C blew our hopes out of the water. He announced that the entire social studies class was going on a field trip after school instead.

To be honest, I'm not sure that standing in the woodsy area behind school can be called a "field trip." There wasn't even a bus to bring us here. We walked.

"This is so depressing," I mumbled under my

breath. I watched a beetle crawl across the ground, but didn't mention it to anyone because I didn't want to have to draw it in our journal.

"Hey, Abigail!" Bo called. Now, he was standing by a pine tree. "Will you please bring me the compass? I need to know which direction this moss is growing."

Groaning, I stepped over the beetle and went to get the compass.

Usually, I'm bold and curious. I like learning and always have a thousand questions about everything. But not today. Today, I was so bored that I thought I might drop dead. They'd write on my tombstone: HERE LIES ABIGAIL KARLIN—BORED TO DEATH.

I glanced over at Zack. He was yawning again. It was odd because Zack is hardly ever bored. Sure, he complains and worries, but even when he's being a pain, he still makes things fun. Zack tells the best jokes. Even his clothes make me laugh. Today, he was wearing torn jeans and a too-big sweatshirt that looked like his firefighter dad had saved it from a burning building.

His twin brother, Jacob, is totally different. Jacob was wearing nice, clean khaki pants and a Hawaiian shirt. Jacob likes learning new things. It surprised me that he wasn't more into the mapping project. I guess if there isn't a computer involved, Jacob isn't going to participate.

I needed something exciting to happen. I desperately looked around for anything to inspire my curiosity and snap me back to being me.

"North!" Bo exclaimed after looking at the compass. "This moss is growing north."

Ugh. Bo's moss wasn't going to do it. I rolled my eyes while Bo took our team journal and excitedly wrote down his discovery.

Mr. C walked up behind me. I didn't see him coming and I nearly jumped out of my skin when he spoke. "It looks like the only one really working in this group is Bo." Mr. C looked at Jacob, Zack, and me with piercing eyes. "Why is that?"

"I—," I began, but stopped. I love Mr. C. He is the best teacher in the whole universe. There was no way

I was going to tell him his cartography project was deadly dull.

But Zack would. "B-O-R-I-N-G." Zack spelled out each letter as if that would make the reason crystal clear.

"Then you'll get a Z-E-R-O," Mr. C responded, pulling his grade book out of his pocket. "Everyone, that is, except Bo."

2
West

"Give us another chance. Please," Jacob begged our teacher. Getting a zero would ruin Jacob's grade. And life.

Mr. C pushed up his glasses. They are always falling down. He thought for a second, tucked his pen into his shirt pocket, closed his grade book, and said, "I think the problem is that you kids simply do not understand why this project is so important."

Bo stopped measuring and came over to listen.

I asked, "Please explain it to us, Mr. Caruthers." Maybe if he gave more details, my curiosity would kick in. I needed to shake off my bored feelings. So far, cartography wasn't even a teenie-weenie bit interesting. There wasn't even one good question rattling in my mind.

But Mr. C had a lot of questions floating around in his brain. "Can you imagine a world without maps?" Mr. C asked us.

"There'd be more trees," Zack joked. "Get it?" He poked me in the arm. "Most maps are on paper, and paper's made of trees."

"I got it," I replied, with a chuckle.

Mr. C flashed us a warning look and asked me to answer his question.

"I suppose," I said, "that it would be harder to get around. We might get lost. Or end up in the wrong place."

"Good, Abigail," Mr. C said. "Now"—he turned to Jacob with the next question—"what if no one had ever been west of this creek?"

I didn't have the compass and wasn't sure which way west was. I glanced at Bo. He pointed out the right direction.

"Hey," Zack said. "We live west of here!" Since I live next door to the twins, I lived west too.

"So," Jacob said thoughtfully, "if no one had ever been west of here, our neighborhood wouldn't exist." After Mr. C nodded, Jacob went on. "And people might be scared to cross the creek because they wouldn't know what was there." Mr. C nodded again. "And people would be crowded over here."

Mr. C smiled. "All true," he said. "Did you know that in 1803, no one from the United States government had officially explored west of the Mississippi River? Most American citizens lived east of that big river." Mr. C looked over at Bo.

Bo was looking down, swinging his foot in the dirt. I knew that it was because he's shy around adults, not because he didn't know the facts.

Bo reads all the time, and remembers everything he reads. "Bo?" Mr. C asked him. "What do you know about the Louisiana Purchase?"

Bo raised his head slightly and answered softly. "In 1803, President Thomas Jefferson bought the territory west of the Mississippi River from the French.

The land doubled the United States' territory. Problem was, no one really knew for sure who lived on the land. Or what kind of land it was."

Mr. C looked so proud, his eyes glowed behind his glasses. Bo sure knew a lot.

Mr. C picked up the story. "President Jefferson knew there were Native Americans living out there. Traders and fur trappers, too. But he only had a few accurate reports. He also thought there were woolly mammoths, unicorns, an erupting volcano, and a great mountain made of salt."

I giggled. "That's crazy!"

Mr. C smiled and raised his eyebrows. "But without having seen the land, President Jefferson didn't know that."

All of a sudden, Jacob remembered something important. "Meriwether Lewis and William Clark," he bubbled. "They were the army captains President Jefferson sent out to explore the land."

"How did you know that?" I asked Jacob. There, I'd asked my first question. It wasn't really a great one, but I was just getting started.

Jacob winked and said, "There's a computer game on the Internet called LC Adventures. The goal is to help Lewis and Clark cross America." He started wiggling his fingers as if he were typing. "You have to follow the Missouri, and Columbia rivers, then cross the Rocky Mountains to get to the Pacific Ocean. The game ends if you starve to death or get killed along the way. You get extra energy points when you correctly use the few supplies President Jefferson gives you at the beginning of the game."

"Sounds like fun," Mr. C commented.

"It is!" Jacob replied. "It's a great game." He paused, then added, "But I've never won. It's really hard."

"Sounds very realistic," Mr. C told us. "In 1803, Lewis and Clark led a group of thirty-three men, called the Corps of Discovery. They set out to see if they could find a river route all the way from Saint Louis, Missouri, to the Pacific Ocean. President Jefferson also wanted them to write down all the plants and animals they saw. And he asked Lewis and Clark to make a map of the new territory."

I sighed and said, "I knew there was a map in this story somewhere."

Mr. C laughed. "Lewis and Clark's journey was all about making a map of the western part of the United States." He looked me in the eyes and added, "Making maps is important work, Abigail."

I knew my teacher was right, but I still didn't want to go back to watching Bo drag the two-pole chain around the creek bed.

Mr. C shivered as he went on with his story. "About eight months into the trip, it was getting cold and the Corps of Discovery needed to spend the winter somewhere. They chose to be near several villages of Hidasta and Mandan Indians and built a fort. While at their fort, Lewis and Clark met Sacagawea."

"Sacaga-who?" Zack asked.

Mr. Caruthers shook his head sadly. "Oh, dear," he moaned. "The school year just isn't long enough."

Jacob flicked Zack on the back of the head. "You're going to get us stuck in summer school, dope."

"I bet you don't know who Sacagawea is either." Zack flicked his brother back on the neck. "Double dope."

"I do too." Jacob bent his fingers into flicking position. "I learned about her from that computer game. She's a character in LC Adventures."

Before another flick could be flicked, Mr. C stepped between the twins. With one hand firmly on each boy's shoulder, he said, "Give me your journal, compass, and two-pole chain. You aren't going to make a map today."

"Yippee," Zack cheered, clapping happily.

"Instead," Mr. C said sternly, "you will be doing a different project."

"Bummer," Zack grumped, stuffing his hands in his pockets.

"What kind of project?" I wondered. My curiosity was finally kicking in.

"When the other groups share their maps, your group will make a presentation about Sacagawea in class tomorrow." Mr. C quickly turned to Bo and said, "I'm certain you've read enough about Sacagawea to make the presentation on your own. You can help, but don't forget, this is a project for the whole group."

Bo stared at the ground and nodded.

"Zack, you got us in trouble!" Jacob gave his brother a mean look. "Now, we're going to be stuck inside the library."

"You can't blame me for not knowing about Sacagawea," Zack argued. "I never played LC Adventures. You never let me play anything on the compu—"

Once again, Mr. C stepped between them before they started fighting. "You aren't going to the library." He reached into his back pocket and pulled out the time-travel computer. Shoving his glasses back up his nose, Mr. C said, "It's time for History Club to begin."

"Hurray!" we all cheered at the same time.

Mr. C handed Jacob the computer and the small cartridge that fit in the back slot. The cartridge had a drawing of a young Native American woman on it. She had a baby strapped to her back.

"Is this Sacagawea?" I asked, pointing at the little picture. "Did Sacagawea quit?"

"Yes," Mr. C said with a long breath. "You are going

to visit Sacagawea. But be prepared because this adventure will definitely be more difficult than the others."

"Why?" I asked. Every question I asked made me feel more and more like my old self. My brain was starting to spin.

Mr. C didn't answer. Instead, he walked us to the back of a large rock where no one else could see us. Jacob slid the cartridge into the computer, and the green glowing time-travel hole opened between the rock and a tree, about four paces away.

Mr. C reminded us that the computer gives us only two hours. When we got back, we'd need to meet up with the field trip so we could all walk back to school together.

Jacob, Zack, and Bo waved good-bye and eagerly jumped into the time-travel hole. Even though the hole was closing, I hung back. Now, curiosity was boiling inside me.

I asked Mr. C again, "Why will this adventure be harder than the others?"

"When you time travel, the famous people you

meet are quitting. You have to convince them to follow their dreams, right?"

"Yeah," I said, carefully watching that the time-travel hole didn't close and leave me behind. "So?"

Mr. C looked at me very seriously. "What would the world be like if Sacagawea quit her dream?"

I considered his question as the green hole shrank a bit more. I wished Jacob and Bo hadn't time-traveled yet. I felt dumb and needed help. I had no clue what the world would be like because, well, I didn't know who Sacagawea was. Or what her dream was.

When I didn't answer, Mr. C took pity on me. "According to my list, Sacagawea is quitting today. You're going to have to figure out who she is and then discover the dream she's giving up." He handed me a sealed envelope. "I hope these will help you convince her not to quit."

As I stuffed the envelope into my pocket, I swore I heard another animal sound. This time, it wasn't a bear growl. No. It was more like little feet scampering across the ground.

Mr. Caruthers didn't seem to notice the sound. I looked around, but didn't see anything.

Then, I heard another noise. Something chewing crunchy leaves. "Did you hear that?" I asked Mr. C.

"Hear what?" he responded.

A second later, I swear a wolf howled. Mr. C didn't react.

When I heard the lion's roar, I didn't care if Mr. C heard it or not. I knew I wasn't curious enough to stick around another second. I didn't want to know what was out there, hiding behind the trees.

Fast as lightning, before the last wisp of smoke floated up from the green hole, I jumped through time.

3

The Shoshone

Well, I definitely wasn't bored anymore.

I landed smack in the middle of a river. The boys were already there, standing in the knee-deep water. Water quickly filled my tennis shoes, soaking my socks and making my jeans feel heavy.

"Yuck," Zack grimaced. "I hate wet feet."

I hated wet feet, too, but I wasn't going to complain. Or groan. Or worry. I'd leave all that to Zack. Right after Mr. C had said we didn't have to do the mapping project, I had snapped back to being my bold and curious self.

Besides, I was in the past, standing in some river. I knew I wasn't anywhere near whatever was making those animal noises. That was good.

Jacob, Zack, and I moved as quickly as we could toward the riverbank. The water wasn't deep, but it was moving fast and felt like melted ice. As I pulled myself out onto the dusty ground, I noticed that Bo was still standing in the water.

"Bo," I called out. "Are you frozen?"

Bo didn't respond. But I could see he was shivering. His sweatpants and T-shirt were totally soaked.

"Bo?" I repeated. "What's the deal? Do you need help?" I was starting to worry.

"Look," he said at last. One word. So soft, I could barely even hear him over the rushing river.

I glanced in the direction he was facing. A large wooden box was floating downstream toward him. And behind that, an empty canoe. It was upside down and moving fast.

The box would pass him by. But in less than a minute, the canoe would sweep Bo off his feet, carrying him away. "Bo!" I shouted, straining my voice. "Get out of the water!"

"I think that's one of Lewis and Clark's canoes!" he called back. "I have to save it."

I quickly turned to the twins. "He's going to get killed. That thing is coming too fast."

Jacob stashed the computer behind a tree, and the three of us jumped into the water. Gritting my teeth against the cold, we lined up next to Bo.

The canoe was practically flying toward us.

Jacob counted: "One. Two." And on three, the middle of the canoe hit me solidly in the thighs, nearly knocking me over. I barely kept my balance, holding on to the canoe with all my might. It dragged me a short ways.

Bo was next to me. He wrapped his hands around the left end of the canoe, trying desperately to slow it down.

Jacob was struggling with the other end. Pushing at it with straight arms.

And Zack was . . . shoot! I didn't see Zack anywhere.

I called out, "Jacob, where's your twin?"

Jacob glanced around, then tilted his head downstream. When we'd gone after the canoe, Zack had reached for the wooden box. He was sort of on top of it, sort of under it. Dragging the crate toward the river's edge.

Bo, Jacob, and I managed to flip the canoe over and get it to the side. We pulled it up onto the riverbank, far enough that the river wouldn't wash it away again. When we were done, we hurried over to Zack.

"Hey, what are you doing?" I called out as we sloshed through the water toward him.

"I'm helping the Quarter Lady," Zack called back.

It was then I noticed the young woman standing with Zack. My sister, CeCe, is sixteen years old. I guessed that this woman was about the same age.

The woman was in the water, pulling on the box, while Zack guided it toward the river's edge. A big hole was in the side of the crate. Loose papers were floating down the river.

By the time Zack and the young woman had gotten the crate wedged on land, Zack was breathless and shivering. Bo, Jacob, and I were also exhausted. I placed my hands on my knees, taking deep breaths.

The woman, though, wasn't resting on the river-bank with us. She'd jumped back into the rushing

water and was sweeping the loose papers into her arms. The papers were totally soaked and moving quickly with the current. It seemed ridiculous to try to save them.

But she was determined to collect as many as she could. Even though her arms were full, she bent to scoop up one more. It was then, as she leaned forward, that we noticed the baby strapped to her back.

"That's Sacagawea!" Bo declared. "Her baby was only two months old when she and her husband joined the Corps of Discovery. They are working as translators for Lewis and Clark."

"Zack," Jacob asked, "if that's Sacagawea, why do you keep calling her 'the Quarter Lady'?"

"I didn't know her name. But still, I recognized her," Zack said matter of factly. "In our time, her face is on gold quarters."

"I've seen those coins, and they're not quarters. They're gold dollars." Jacob sighed. "That would make her the Dollar Lady, you spaz."

"Same size as a quarter. Same shape as a quarter.

Looks like a quarter to me," Zack claimed. "And I'm not a spaz, you are."

I'd have yelled at them both to cut it out, but Bo calmly told the twins, "Sacagawea and her baby are pictured on a dollar coin," he explained. "But dollar coins have never been popular. No one ever uses them. I think dollar coins are too easily confused with quarters."

"See?" Zack chuckled. "I was kind of right."

"That means I was kind of right too," Jacob said, smiling.

Sacagawea was struggling to pull papers from the rushing water. Her dress was sopping wet. It looked like it was made of animal skin. There were wet feathers in her hair.

"We can't stand here while she does all the work." Bo headed back toward the river. "We have to help."

Wet and cold, we all followed Bo.

A tall, thin man appeared suddenly, blocking our way. "Stop!" the man commanded. "We have saved all that we can." He called to Sacagawea, whistling and waving his arms to get her attention. She immediately climbed out of the water, carrying the papers she'd collected.

Sacagawea set the papers out to dry along the shore, securing them with rocks. When she finished, the man told her to go back downstream. He didn't actually use any words to explain; rather, he pointed to her dress and to the baby, indicating that she should change them both into dry clothes.

Sacagawea didn't speak. She simply nodded and walked away.

Soaked, tired, and freezing cold, Bo, Jacob, Zack, and I all collapsed down on the ground. We were exhausted and needed to relax in the warm sun.

Standing over us, the man said, "My own men ran away, afraid to be pulled downriver by the current. Not one of them attempted to get the canoe, the papers, or the supply box from the water. You and Sacagawea saved many important things today." There was sincere gratitude in his voice when he said, "Thank you."

"You're welcome," Zack replied. "But could you move left slightly? You're blocking my rays."

The man chuckled and took a step to the side. "Who are you and where are you from?" he asked. "We have not seen other people in weeks. Not even Indians."

I wanted to tell him that, in our time, we didn't use the word "Indians." We use the phrase "Native Americans" because the tribes didn't come from anywhere else. They were some of the first people in this country.

Bo gave me a look that said he knew what I was thinking and that I should let it go. In 1805 the word "Indian" was the right word. So, I told the man our names instead.

Then, I began to say, "We came from the fut—" when Jacob cut me off.

"TMI," Jacob interrupted.

I knew what that meant. Too Much Information. Jacob was trying to say that I shouldn't go around telling people about the time-travel machine. We'd just tell Sacagawea. And then, only if it would help us to convince her to . . . to not quit whatever she was quitting.

Bo tipped a finger toward the man and mouthed, "Captain Clark."

"That's Captain Clark?" Zack asked softly, and Bo confirmed it with a strong nod.

William Clark was wearing an old-fashioned United States Army jacket like I'd seen in movies. There were medals and stripes across the front, and down the sleeves.

"So, you were about to tell me where you came from," Captain Clark said, his red hair glistening in the sunlight.

"We're from over there." Jacob pointed over his shoulder with his thumb. Behind us, towering in the distance, were huge mountains. There was snow covering the peaks.

"Yeah," I confirmed. "We came from that way." Then, I leaned over and whispered to Jacob, "Where are we exactly?"

Jacob looked at the computer screen and read, "'Montana. August 17th, 1805.'"

"I knew that was the Bitterroot Range," Bo said. "It is the northernmost part of the great Rocky

Mountains." Bo's face shone with excitement as he added, "I've been to Montana before."

At Bo's words, Captain Clark squinted his eyes to get a better look at us. "Are you certain you are from this part of the west?"

I sat up and shrugged. I was feeling too wet and wiped out to make up a whole, big story, so I said simply, "We've come to meet Sacagawea."

"Ahh," Captain Clark said. "So her fame has reached these lands. Janey is an important member of this expedition. We couldn't have come this far without her."

"Who's Janey?" I whispered to Bo. But before Bo could answer, Captain Clark said, "Here come Janey and Pomp now."

I figured that Janey must be the nickname William Clark had for Sacagawea since she was the only one headed toward us.

Bo leaned over and told me that Sacagawea's baby's real name was Jean-Baptiste, but William Clark called him Pomp. Sacagawea and Pomp were both wearing dry clothes. She was moving very slowly, carrying a large pile in her arms.

While we waited for her to arrive, William Clark asked, "Have you seen Captain Meriwether Lewis?" There was a troubled look in his eyes. "Captain Lewis said he would set up camp near here, but we haven't found him yet. It is my fault that we are late. By now, he must be worried."

"We haven't seen him," I responded. "Why are you so late?"

Captain Clark replied, "A few days ago, Lewis and I discovered that a boat cannot sail the whole way to the Pacific Ocean. The river is too shallow. Captain Lewis left me with our canoes and most of the Corps of Discovery. He took a few men with him. They went to find the Shoshone tribe. We must buy some horses from them. We are going to have to ride through those mountains to continue our journey westward."

He pointed at the landscape and sighed. "The Rocky Mountains are not at all what we expected.

When we began our expedition, we looked at an old map a trapper had drawn of this area. The map showed just one, small, easy-to-climb hill."

I laughed thinking about how really bad the old maps were: Woolly mammoths, erupting volcanoes, and one little hill. I looked at the huge range of mountains before us. The peaks reached up to the sky, and the hills went on and on as far as my eyes could see.

President Jefferson really needed Lewis and Clark's new map. "Good thing you're here," I told William Clark.

"Yes. We will definitely add these mountains to our new map."

"New map?" I repeated, and suddenly I realized what we were doing. I turned to Bo and asked, "Meeting Sacagawea is all about mapmaking isn't it?" I felt a little like Mr. C had tricked me. I had hoped when we left the field trip we were done with cartography, but the fact was, meeting Sacagawea was also going to be about making maps.

Bo asked, "Would you have come if I had told you this adventure was about making maps?"

"I don't know—" I stopped and thought about it. "Of course I would have come. Even if they are boring, maps are part of American history," I admitted. "And it's our job to save history."

Zack laughed and said, "Well, at least we aren't the ones who have to draw it."

Captain Clark clearly had no clue what we were talking about. He shook his head and went on. "I shall also record in my journal that the river through this area is very shallow. I thought it looked deep enough to try to float a canoe and some of our supplies."

Captain Clark looked down and bit his lip sadly. "I was wrong. The canoe hit a rock and overturned. If you children had not caught the boat—" He sighed deeply and started a different thought. "Well, it is a good thing Captain Lewis is out looking for horses. Obviously, we cannot travel in the water anymore, at all."

Just as I began to say that I was glad we didn't have to go through the mountains with them, Sacagawea arrived. "These are for you and your friends," she said, handing me the pile she was carrying. "Take these dry clothes and change."

I said, "Thank you," but she didn't seem to understand me, so instead I smiled really big and accepted the clothing.

The boys were staring, totally confused, at the pile in my arms. They must not have been paying attention. I explained that Sacagawea had brought us dry clothes.

After passing out the items, we all scattered into the bushes to get dressed. When we returned, we were each wearing adult-size army uniforms and beaded, leather moccasins. We were carrying our wet things.

Down by the river, Sacagawea was going nuts. She was singing and dancing and waving her hands in the air.

"What is going on?" Zack asked. "We weren't gone even one whole minute!"

We noticed that the men from the Corps of Discovery had caught up. They were carrying heavy loads of equipment, canoes, and boxes of supplies. But that wasn't why Sacagawea was excited.

In the opposite direction from the Corps, several Native-American men rode toward us on horseback. Each man had a bow in his hand and a basket of arrows slung over his back.

Rushing toward the Native Americans, Sacagawea was shouting with joy, "At last. At last. My people. We have found my people!"

4

Camp Fortunate

"What is Sacagawea doing?" Zack asked as we all followed the Native Americans and their horses. They knew where Meriwether Lewis had set up camp. "She keeps on yelling, dancing, and running in circles. Boy, she's acting strange."

"What's wrong with you, Zack!?" I wondered if he should have his hearing checked. "Aren't you listening? Sacagawea says she found her people. She's happy."

It was no wonder why Jacob fought so much with Zack. I felt like arguing with him too. Frustrated, I turned to Bo and asked, "You heard her, right?"

"Abigail, you can't possibly know what she's saying because she's speaking in Shoshone." Bo looked at me like I was loopy.

"What are you talking about? She's speaking English. I understand every single word—" Even as I said it, I knew how I had understood. I stopped walking. "Sorry guys," I apologized.

In my hand was the envelope Mr. C had given me before I time-traveled. It was wet and soggy. I had taken it out of my jeans pocket when I changed clothes. I held the envelope up into the sunlight.

"What's that?" Jacob asked.

"Mr. C gave me this envelope," I explained, ripping open the sealed flap. "He said this would help us figure out Sacagawea's dream."

Inside were five bright blue, flat stones. I dumped them into my hand. Engraved on each stone was a picture: One had an antelope. Another a mountain lion. The third one had a raccoon on it. A coyote was carved on the fourth. On the last one was a bear.

"I think these stones helped me understand Sacagawea." I randomly dropped one stone into each boy's hand. There were two left, so I took one and I stuck the last one in the pocket of my borrowed army jacket.

"These must be translators!" Jacob cheered. He turned it over in his hand, inspecting it. "Mr. C is a great inventor. I bet there's a mini computer chip hidden in here somewhere."

"Don't take it apart to find out," Zack warned his brother.

"All I know is that when I was holding the envelope with the stones," I said, "I could understand Sacagawea like she was talking in plain English."

Bo rubbed his chin and said, "But when you spoke to her, thanking her for the clothes, she clearly didn't understand you." He was thinking hard. "We are going to have to figure out how to talk to her."

"We can swallow it," Jacob suggested, rolling the blue stone between his fingers. "Maybe then we'll be able to speak Shoshone."

"It might get lodged in our throat. We could choke and die." Zack held his hands over his throat and began gagging. "The stones might be made of toxic materials. We'd be poisoned and die."

I didn't think we'd die, but I really didn't want to swallow the stone either.

We were trying to figure another way to talk to Sacagawea when Captain Clark interrupted. He invited us to come meet the Shoshone chief.

"There must be a way to use these so that she can understand us," Jacob mumbled as we followed William Clark to a large, open area downstream. "It's like a little computer," he said, turning the stone over and over in his palm, trying to figure out how it worked.

In a grassy place, the Corps of Discovery had made a tent by tying a boat sail to a tall bush. Under the shade, a Native-American man was seated on a white robe spread on the ground. Captain Clark introduced us to him. He was Chief Cameahwait.

Captain Clark pointed out Sacagawea's husband, a French trapper named Toussaint Charbonneau. Then we shook hands with the Corps translator, François Labiche.

Finally, William Clark introduced us to Captain Meriwether Lewis. Captain Lewis was tall and thin like Captain Clark. He had grayish hair and was very tan. I guessed that he spent most of his days outside.

A black dog lay sleeping near Captain Lewis. "The dog's called Seaman," Bo explained in a whisper. "He belongs to Captain Lewis. I read that he traveled the whole way to the Pacific Ocean and back again."

"Where's Sacagawea?" I asked Bo as we laid our clothes out to dry and joined the group under the shade.

"Here she comes," Jacob said, pointing as Sacagawea and the baby Pomp joined us.

As Sacagawea went to sit down next to her husband, she paused, staring at Chief Cameahwait. I figured it was because she had missed the introduction and didn't know his name, but she never asked who he was. In fact, she didn't talk at all. She just kept staring at the Shoshone chief.

Captain Clark explained that François Labiche would translate English into French. Toussaint Charbonneau would convert the French words to Hidatsa. And Sacagawea would change the Hidatsa to Shoshone for the chief.

Then, Captain Lewis began the meeting. "This land now belongs to the United States of America."

"How much time do we have?" Zack whispered to Jacob as each person in the translation chain told the next one what Lewis had said. "This could take hours."

Jacob leaned over and whispered, "We have one hour, eleven minutes. Plenty of time."

For some reason, I didn't understand when Sacagawea spoke in Shoshone or Hidatsa. I figured maybe the stones only worked when we talked to her directly. That was fine. The human translation chain worked so well, we didn't need the stones to help us know what was going on.

Captain Lewis explained that the tribes were now governed by a great man in the far east named President Thomas Jefferson. He gave the Shoshone chief a small coin-size medal with a picture of Jefferson on one side and two hands shaking on the other. He called it a peace medal.

The chief rose and tied white shells in William Clark's red hair. He also put some in Lewis's gray-streaked hair. They looked like little pearls. When the chief sat again, he passed a peace pipe around.

Once the men had smoked the pipe, the trading began.

Sacagawea was staring at Chief Cameahwait again while William Clark explained that the usual price was one knife for one horse. He put his own knife down on the blanket so everyone could see it. Sacagawea didn't look at the knife. I guess she'd seen one a thousand times. She just kept looking at the chief.

The chief picked up the knife and inspected it. Then he said, "My tribe is the poorest of the nations. We are constantly raided by other Indian tribes with guns. They get their weapons from the east. From trappers and other travelers. The Shoshone need guns for hunting and to protect ourselves."

He paused for the translators to catch up, then said, "Five years ago, the Hidatsa Indians raided our tribe. They stole Shoshone horses. They even kidnapped many of our people. They took my sister away. Of my family, only my nephew and I survived."

Suddenly, Sacagawea began to weep. She leaped up from her place, a flood of Shoshone words coming from her mouth, and rushed over to the chief. He grasped her by the shoulders, looked clearly into her face, and broke into a mighty grin. Sacagawea then wrapped her blanket around his shoulders. Pressing her face into his neck, Sacagawea began to cry in loud, heartfelt sobs.

The Shoshone chief wrapped her into a hug and we knew right away that he was someone special. For a long time, Chief Cameahwait held her close. Sacagawea cried and cried some more. Finally, she lifted her head and spoke to her husband, Charbonneau.

The translation went down the line until François Labiche announced that Sacagawea was the sister in Chief Cameahwait's story. She had been kidnapped as a girl, and now, after all these years apart, Sacagawea was finally reunited with her brother!

My cheeks hurt from holding back my own happy tears.

Captain Lewis declared, "Because of the reunion between Sacagawea and her brother Chief Cameahwait, we will forever call this place Camp Fortunate.

We are very fortunate to have found Sacagawea's brother, alive and well."

Bo cupped his mouth with his hand and said, "That's how most of the places Lewis and Clark visited got names. They named them after people on the trip or things that happened. It's a bummer, but most of those names were changed later by explorers."

When the trading finally ended, it was agreed that the Shoshone would receive a knife, a gun, and some bullets for each horse. In exchange, the explorers would get twenty-nine horses and a Shoshone guide to help them across the Rocky Mountains.

The Native Americans would also get clothing and extra food after they gave Lewis and Clark information about the mountains for this part of their map.

Everyone seemed happy that it was a fair trade.

Everyone, that is, except Bo.

"What's up?" I asked Bo, who had an incredibly sad look on his face.

"The Shoshone agree to the trade now, because they want the guns. They have never seen the white people before. They are excited. But, truthfully, they have no idea what is going to happen in the near future."

"What do you mean?" Jacob wondered.

"Well," Bo explained, "Lewis and Clark thought that other U.S. government explorers would bring the promised guns and knives to the Shoshone. But that won't happen. In fact, when the explorers and settlers come across America, the Shoshone and all Native Americans will be gathered up and sent to live in camps called Indian Reservations. They won't be able to move around freely like they do now. They'll be stuck with some of the worst land in America."

"Really?" Zack asked. "Are you sure? The Shoshone don't seem afraid of what will happen. They're still talking happily about the trade."

"I'm positive," Bo told us. "Even in our time, there are still Reservations. Many Native Americans are very poor. And they have lost much of their special culture." He sighed. "Truthfully, Lewis and Clark don't know what is going to happen either. In a few years,

Captain Lewis will become very sad when he realizes how unfairly the Native Americans are treated."

Bo paused for a second, then added, "Did I mention that the settlers are also going to kill most of the buffalo, cut down many of the forests, build railroads, and create big cities all over the west? Some people think that cities are really good. Others people think cities destroy the land and animals."

I wasn't sure what I thought about building cities. I mean, I like going to the mall, more than I like camping. Then again, I know trees and fresh air are healthy, and it was beautiful around here. . . .

Hmmm. I'd have to think about cities versus nature when I got back home. Right now, I was more worried about what was going to happen to the Native Americans.

"Should we warn Chief Cameahwait?" I asked Bo.

We both looked over at the Shoshone chief. He seemed so pleased with the details of the trade. He was happy to have found his sister. We knew it wasn't our job to change history. Just to keep it on track. Besides, Chief Cameahwait seemed so excited about the trade, he wouldn't have believed us anyway.

Calling everyone to attention, Captain Lewis declared, "Now we must talk about the map."

We all went outside the sail-shade. There, by the side of the river, Captain Lewis asked one of his men to get their mapping equipment.

Bo's face lit up when the man returned with a two-pole chain and compass.

Zack rolled his eyes and looked bored as William Clark got out his personal journal and began to make notations. They were measuring distances—from Camp Fortunate to the river. The river to the tall reeds nearby. Reeds to rocks. And once those numbers were collected, Captain Clark asked Chief Cameahwait to draw a picture of the mountains using a stick in the dirt.

Chief Cameahwait built the mountain range out of sand. He was just about to draw a trail with his stick when two men on horseback came riding into camp. They were wearing U.S. Army jackets, but didn't have nearly as many medals and stripes as either Lewis or Clark.

"We borrowed some horses from the tribe and went off to kill a deer for you as a gift for your people," one of the riders announced. "We shot one just over that ridge." The translators scrambled to tell the Chief Cameahwait what the soldier was saying.

Chief Cameahwait immediately threw down his drawing stick. "It is time to eat," he declared. "We will make the map later."

"But we need it now," Clark insisted.

Lewis added, "It is of great importance to us."

"Food first. Map later." Chief Cameahwait walked away.

5

Dreams

"Wait!" William Clark called after Chief Cameah-wait. "The map!" But it was no use. The chain of translation had been broken. Even Sacagawea and her husband had hurried after the others toward the dead deer.

There were about sixty Native Americans plus the thirty-three men in the Corps, all rushing toward the ridge. We followed to see what was going to happen.

The Native Americans sped past on horseback. The members of the Corps had to walk, since they didn't have horses. We walked too. By the time we arrived, the deer had been torn limb from limb.

We stood with Lewis and Clark's men and watched

as the Native Americans sat on the ground hunched over, eating the deer raw.

I felt sick. "Couldn't they have waited for the barbecue?" I asked the boys, turning my head away. I couldn't watch.

"They're starving," Bo responded. I refused to peek, shutting my eyes tightly, so Bo described the scene. "The Shoshone are eating like they haven't had meat in a very long time. I remember reading that the Shoshone were so poor, there were times when they ate nothing but berries for months."

"I hate berries," Zack commented as he watched one man eat. Zack told me there was fresh blood dripping down the man's chin. He described how the man wiped his face on his arm and kept eating.

"Eeww," I said, holding my stomach. I took a quick glance at Jacob. He was a nice bright shade of green.

"Starting today, I'm a vegetarian," he declared.

When the deer meat was gone, two Native-American men lent two Corps soldiers their horses. The soldiers took their rifles and rode off to hunt another deer.

The people in Lewis and Clark's Corps of Discovery weren't starving like the Native Americans. They hunted and fished, but they also had brought dried food and other supplies with them. Today's lunch was dried buffalo meat and some roots that Sacagawea had dug up herself.

While everyone ate, Zack, Jacob, Bo, and I decided we'd better go find Sacagawea. We only had fifty-two minutes left on the computer and we hadn't talked to her at all. Except for that tiny conversation when she handed me the clothes.

"Everything seems fine," Zack remarked. "I haven't heard anything about Sacagawea quitting." He scratched at his neck. "Maybe after we talk to her, we can change back to our wet clothes and zoom home. These army uniforms itch."

Sacagawea was over by the river. The Corps of Discovery had brought the rest of their gear and stashed it in big piles by the river's edge.

She was leaning over an open crate, taking items and stuffing them into a small carrying bag. Sacagawea was singing a Native-American chant while she worked. I don't know why, but even though I had the translator stone in my hand, I didn't understand her song.

Crossing over to her, I said, "You must be very happy to have found your brother again."

Sacagawea stopped packing, but didn't stop chanting. She looked up at me and shook her head. It was obvious that she didn't know what I was saying.

I opened my hand, revealing my translator stone inside.

I had an idea. Reaching out, I took her hand and shared my translator stone by setting it in her palm.

"Are you happy to find your brother?" I asked again.

She looked down at the stone in her hand, turning it round and round, examining it.

"It doesn't work," I told the boys, taking the stone back from her.

The stone I held had the antelope carved on it.

"Trade me," I said to Zack. "Maybe the antelope is broken."

Zack's stone had the raccoon picture engraved on it. The very second I held the stone, the words to

Sacagawea's native chant became clear in my head. As clear as if she were singing in English.

"It works," I exclaimed. "We were holding the wrong stones." I pulled the bear stone out of my pocket. "Mine is the raccoon, but who gets which one of the others?"

We all stood together, holding the stones before us in our open palms.

Sacagawea came and peered over my shoulder, interested in what we were doing. The boys were switching stones again and again, trying to match up with the right ones.

Sacagawea shook her head at them and held out her hand, silently requesting the boys give her all the stones. I kept mine, so I was the only one who understood her words.

"The spirits of animals stand beside each of you. You"—she pointed at me—"are like the raccoon, curious and full of wonder."

Turning to Jacob, she handed him the antelope stone. Suddenly, Jacob's eyes brightened and I knew he understood what Sacagawea was saying. "Your spirit is the antelope, the one who takes action."

She handed Zack his stone. "There is a coyote beside you. A cunning trickster. The master of humor. Even though you have a strong survival instinct, you howl at the moon. Full of worry." Zack proudly smiled because the description fit perfectly.

"And you"—she gave a blue stone to Bo—"you stand with the mountain lion. Swift with wisdom and balanced in leadership."

I wondered how she was able to figure us out so fast. Were there really animal spirits hovering around us? I felt a cold chill travel down my spine and I remembered the sounds I had heard just before time-traveling.

"The raccoon, antelope, coyote, and mountain lion are animal spirits who protect and guide you." Sacagawea looked down at the last stone in her hand and asked, "But who is the bear?"

In the flash of an instant, I knew the answer to Sacagawea's question. "You are the bear," I said confidently. Sacagawea stared at me as if I were nutty, and yet she definitely understood what I had said.

The bear stone had worked. It had translated for her. So, I asked her to explain what the spirit of the bear meant.

"The bear spirit walks with a person who has many dreams and the brave strength to follow those desires."

"Yep," I exclaimed. "The bear stone is yours—for sure." I told her my name and introduced the boys.

Now that we understood one another, it was time for business. "Sacagawea," Jacob asked, "since you are the bear, what is your dream?"

Sacagawea looked down at the stone in her hand and said, "I have no dreams of my own." She didn't sound sad. She was just stating a fact. "I do not walk with the spirit of the bear. There is no animal spirit beside me."

She looked up at the sound of her name. "My brother is calling. I must finish packing my things," she said, handing me back the bear stone.

"Where are you going?" I asked, refusing to take the translator, practically forcing her to keep the stone.

"I am running away. I have decided to follow Chief Cameahwait and the Shoshone tribe to the buffalo hunting grounds. The buffalo are on the move—we must leave Camp Fortunate immediately." Sacagawea sighed.

"What about Lewis and Clark?" Jacob sounded panicked. "You have to help them on the rest of their journey!"

"Lewis and Clark do not need me," she replied, head hung low. "The Corps of Discovery will find their way."

"You can't just pack up and go!" I cried out. "You're married! What about your husband?" If she wouldn't stay to help Lewis and Clark, maybe she'd stay with Charbonneau.

"He'll be fine without me too." Sacagawea shrugged, then looked me straight in the eye and said, "I have no reason to stay. You cannot stop me. I quit."

And with those words, she handed me the bear stone and refused to take it again.

6

Buffalo

"Maybe we should jump back to school now," Zack suggested. "Sacagawea just quit. She says she has no dream. And this stupid uniform is giving me a rash." Zack scratched at his arm.

"Maybe you could stop scratching for a second and we can help Sacagawea find her dream," Jacob replied. "If she had a dream of her own, maybe she wouldn't quit."

Mr. C was right. This adventure was way more difficult than any of our others. Usually, the people we visited were quitting their dreams. How could we help Sacagawea follow her dream if she didn't have one? And what if her dream was something she wanted to do without Lewis and Clark?

"I don't know how you get someone a dream," I said. "Isn't a dream something people think up on their own? It's what they really want and what they hope and—"

Suddenly, Bo interrupted. "Maps!" he said so loudly, I jumped in surprise. "How could I have forgotten it's all about maps? I hate to say it," he admitted, "but it kind of doesn't matter if Sacagawea has her own dream. For history to stay on track, we need to convince her to stay and help Lewis and Clark finish their map."

We all agreed to try. Still, in my heart, I hoped that while we were convincing Sacagawea to stay with the expedition, she'd also find a dream of her own.

I went over to Sacagawea and begged her to take the bear stone, saying, "Please, we can't talk to you if you don't hold the stone." I had to repeat myself a few times before she finally took back the rock.

Bo looked at Sacagawea and said seriously, "Lewis and Clark wouldn't have made it this far without you." Sacagawea was just a teenager, not quite a real adult, but it was still tough for shy Bo to talk to her.

"Yes, they would have," Sacagawea claimed. She was only half-listening, playing with the beads on her dress. "They don't need me."

"Yes, they do," Bo insisted. I heard him mutter the word "maps" under his breath as he built up the courage to go on.

"A few months ago, some of the boats overturned on the river," he reminded her. "It was kind of like what happened today, only the water was colder and deeper. Many of the men were too afraid to go into the rushing water, but you risked your life to help save the expedition's mapping journals and supplies."

I gave Bo a big thumbs-up. Sacagawea might not be convinced, but she'd stopped looking at her beads. She was definitely listening.

Bo continued: "Later, when you were so sick, everyone thought you'd die, Captain Lewis took care of you, giving you medicine until you got healthy."

"See?" I said, helping Bo. "Lewis wouldn't have spent so much time nursing you if you weren't important."

Jacob chimed in, telling Sacagawea, "After you got healthy, you traveled to a place where two rivers came together. You knew the correct river to take. You led the Corps of Discovery to the Shoshone lands and to Camp Fortunate. Without you, they might have gotten lost." He smiled at me and whispered, "That's part of the computer game."

"Are you convinced how important you are?" I asked her. "Without your translation, Lewis and Clark cannot make their map. They'll never reach the ocean." I couldn't believe I was honestly trying to convince Sacagawea to help make a map. My, how things had changed!

A light glinted in her eyes at the word "ocean," but it passed so quickly, I wasn't sure if it was real or if I'd imagined it.

"Don't forget about Chief Cameahwait," Zack added, scratching at his arms. "It's also important that you convince your brother to stay at Camp Fortunate awhile longer. Even though the trade is complete, Chief Cameahwait still needs to help Lewis and Clark find a route over the mountains."

He winked and said, "It's all about the map, right?"

Without even thinking about our words, Sacagawea quickly replied, "All this makes little difference to me." She opened her hand, revealing the bear-carved stone. "I am going to the buffalo grounds with my brother and my people. We are leaving as soon as possible."

I tried to be understanding about what it must be like for her to finally have a chance to be with her brother and her people after all these years. But still, my own hopes were squashed. Jacob, Zack, Bo, and I had given it our best shot, and failed.

"I wish her brother hadn't asked her to come with him," I moaned to the boys.

Sacagawea, still holding the bear stone in her hand, overheard me and said, "Chief Cameahwait did not tell me to come with him. I told him I wanted to go."

"What!?" Zack exclaimed.

"Even though I was reunited with my brother, I had planned to stay with the expedition. But that woman over there"—Sacagawea pointed at a shadowy figure lurking between the trees—"convinced me to go hunt the buffalo with my tribe." Sacagawea finally handed me her bear stone and went back to gathering her belongings for her trip.

I looked over at the woman standing in the shadows. There was something vaguely familiar about her yellow hat and matching coat.

I'd seen that coat and hat before. But where?

7

Babs Magee

"That's the woman who opened the door to the Presidential Palace in 1862," Bo exclaimed. "We saw her again in New York City in 1928."

"I remember her from Boston in 1876," Jacob realized. "And—"

"She was on the Edmund Pettus Bridge in 1965," Zack finished. "I think she's following us! Or are we following her?"

"Definitely way too many coincidences." I was bouncing on my toes, ready to run. "Let's go get her. We have to find out who she is and what she's up to!"

Sacagawea was still packing as we ran, fast as we could, toward the woman. She saw us coming and took off. Darting through small trees. Ducking behind bushes.

Zack was the quickest, so he was in the lead. Bo was second. I came third. And Jacob, desperately clinging to the computer, careful not to drop it as he ran, was bringing up the rear.

I slowed slightly to jump over a pile of leaves. Coming too fast, Jacob crashed into me. Arms flailing, wrapped together, the two of us plowed into Bo. He slammed into Zack. And Zack . . . well, he cruised headfirst into the woman with the yellow coat and matching hat.

"At least I managed to save the time-travel computer," Jacob grunted from the top of our tangled-people pile. He held it high above his head. "Not a scratch on it."

I looked at the computer in his hand. "That's not our computer," I said, shaking my head. "Ours is black. The one you're holding is blue."

"Give me back my computer," came a shout from beneath Zack. It was the woman in yellow. Her hand shot up and snatched the computer out of Jacob's grasp.

"Excellent. Now, I have two!" she cheered. And with that, Jacob, Zack, Bo, and I were shoved aside as the woman dug herself out from under us. "So long, kids," she said happily as she tucked our computer into her pocket and began to fiddle with the buttons on hers.

Jacob suddenly shouted, "She's going to time-travel out of here!"

"She's taking our computer," Bo added.

"We have to stop her!" Zack cried.

Those three months Zack spent in tae kwon do really paid off when he gave the woman a swift side kick, forcing her to her knees. The summer he spent as a magician's apprentice taught him how to pick our computer from her pocket. And baseball camp scored with a pitcher's perfect toss to Jacob.

Jacob caught our computer easily and declared, "Way to go, Zack. You're a stud."

"I know." Zack grinned. But he didn't have time to take a bow because the woman was back on her feet, preparing to run.

There was no way I was going to let her escape.

Without thinking, I leaped onto her back and hung on.

She couldn't work her own time-travel computer because she was busy swatting at me. And I wasn't going to let go. "Who are you?" I demanded to know. I wrapped my arms tightly around her neck.

Bo and Zack jumped in, grabbing the woman's arms. Jacob kept his distance so she couldn't break free and take our computer again.

She suddenly stopped fighting and stood defeated, breathing heavily. "My name is Babs Magee," she coughed out. I was choking her. I loosened my grip, but wouldn't let go or get off. "Have you heard of me?"

"No," I said. "Should we have?"

"That's the whole problem." Babs sighed. "No one has ever heard of me. But someday I will be very, very famous. Everyone will know the name Babs Magee." She straightened her back. I had to hold on more firmly so I wouldn't slide off.

"Many years ago, I was Mr. C's assistant," she explained. "I helped him create Big Blue."

I remembered that a while back, Mr. C told us he had invented an earlier model of the time-travel computer. He'd painted the front blue and named it Big Blue. Mr. Caruthers thought that Big Blue had been lost on his way back from 1776. He'd invented a new and better computer to replace it. We used this new computer.

"Mr. C didn't lose Big Blue. You stole it," Jacob accused.

"Yes, I did!" she shouted proudly. "I took it because Big Blue is the key to my dream. I want to be famous. To make my dream come true, all I have to do is convince just one famous American to quit for good. Then, I'll finish up his or her work and take all the glory. Very soon, you'll read about ME in your history books at school!"

"You actually go back in time, telling people it would be better if they gave up?" Bo's jaw was gaping open. I could see that he was totally shocked.

"Exactly," Babs admitted as if this were the world's most perfect plan. "Quitting is much easier than trying again and again."

Now I understood why everyone in Mr. C's little black book of names was quitting. She must have a copy of that list and was going down it, visiting one name every Monday, trying to convince him or her to give up so she could take over. I'd never met anyone like Babs Magee.

"You're lazy! You can't get famous by taking someone else's dream," I insisted.

"Why not?" she asked me. But before I could answer, Babs said, "I thought I did it once. No one has ever heard of the Smacktell because I convinced the inventor, James Smooter, to quit. Thing is, I couldn't figure out how to work the stupid Smacktell myself. I didn't get the fame for that one. But now, if you kids will just stop meddling, I know I can become famous today." She tossed her shoulders a bit, trying to throw me off. I hung on tightly.

Babs kept talking. "Since Sacagawea doesn't have a dream of her own, it was simple to convince her to quit the expedition. I spent a whole month learning how to say 'Go with your brother' in Shoshone. And it worked! Now, I will lead Lewis and Clark across the Rocky Mountains. In the future, you'll see my face on a gold quarter."

I mumbled, "One-dollar coin," just as Jacob and Zack shouted, "Get your own life!" in twin-time.

"No!" Babs screamed, and then, she twisted her body around with all her might. Bo and Zack lost their balance and both boys tumbled backward. Babs Magee swung her body right. Then left. Then right again. And I fell off her back.

She dashed away into the shadows, and called out from a place we could not see, "Someday, everyone will know the name BABS MAGEE!"

"What should we do?" I asked the boys. "Should we try to find her?"

Checking his watch, Jacob warned, "We only have twenty-two minutes left before we have to go back to school." He looked really concerned. Twenty-two minutes wasn't very much time!

"Forget about Babs for now," Bo said, making a quick decision. "I have a plan." He turned to Jacob. "Can you program the computer to take us to Sioux Falls, South Dakota, in our own time?"

"Wouldn't you rather go to NASA?" Jacob replied, clearly in sync with whatever Bo was thinking.

Bo brushed off Jacob's idea with a swipe of his hand. "NASA already sent most of the SRTM data to USGS EROS."

"Well, if you're sure." Jacob looked down at the computer. Bo said he was positive, and Jacob began pressing buttons.

I glanced down at the translator stone in my hand. I shook it. Jacob and Bo were speaking English, and yet I didn't understand one single word.

I turned to Zack. "Did you get any of that?"

"Only that we're going to South Dakota." Zack raised his shoulders. "Sometimes it's hard to believe that Jacob and I share the same mom and dad. He's a mutant geek."

"That makes Bo a mutant geek too. He understands me better than my own twin," Jacob said with a laugh. Bo blushed. There was a hot pink stripe across his cheeks.

Taking pity on Zack and me, Jacob explained, "NASA is the National Aeronautics and Space

Administration. They're the part of the government that leads space exploration."

Bo chimed in, saying, "In 2000, the Space Shuttle Endeavor carried a special type of radar that could take measurements of the earth. As the Shuttle traveled around the earth, it collected information called data."

"I thought the data was still at NASA," Jacob picked up from there. "But Bo swears that the information from the Shuttle Radar Topography Mission, SRTM, is now being analyzed in South Dakota. It's at a United States Geological Survey site called the USGS EROS Data Center. EROS stands for Earth Resources Observation System."

"So," I asked, "how will showing Sacagawea the SR-thingy convince her to translate for Lewis and Clark?"

"Trust me," Bo said. "Remember, it's all about making maps."

"Okay, I trust you," I replied as we hurried toward Sacagawea.

"I don't know why we need to show Sacagawea

someone making maps," Zack began. "Seems to me she sees William Clark draw boring maps every single day." He paused, then added, "But I don't have a better idea. And you aren't leaving me here with Crazy Babs Magee."

We rushed over and caught up with Sacagawea just in time. She was ready to meet up with her brother and the rest of the Shoshone tribe.

I grabbed her hand and shoved the bear carved stone in her palm, saying, "We need you to come with us."

"No," she replied. "It's time for me to go." The baby on her back was wide-eyed and awake. "The buffalo—," she began.

"Are big and fat and move slowly," Zack finished.

"They'll still be there when we get back," Jacob put in. And without waiting for her response, or even going to a private spot, Jacob quickly removed the cartridge from the computer. The green glowing hole opened in the dirt, right beside us.

Sacagawea stepped back, a look of fear on her face.

I took her arm, saying, "If you can jump into a

freezing river, this will be easy." She let me lead her toward the hole.

Bo took her other arm.

"We will come right back?" Sacagawea asked us. "Very soon?"

"Yes," I promised. And before she could change her mind or run away, Jacob and Zack joined hands with us.

On the count of three we jumped and on four we landed.

Because time travel is really fast.

8

Mapmaking

We landed in a long hallway at the United States Geological Survey EROS Data Center in Sioux Falls, South Dakota.

When we told Sacagawea where we were, her eyes darkened. "I am afraid," she admitted.

"Is it the time travel?" Jacob asked. "Are you scared about the future?"

"Native Americans believe in all the mysteries of the world. If you say we passed through time, I believe you." Sacagawea wrapped her arms around her waist and shivered. "It is the Sioux Indians I fear. I have never met the Sioux, but I hear they are a mighty tribe."

I would have laughed had she not looked so

serious. "Sacagawea," I explained, "yes, the Sioux are a tribe, but we aren't visiting them. We are at a special place in a city called Sioux Falls."

She nodded, still cautious, but her face appeared calmer. "We cannot keep my brother waiting," she said at last. "Show me this special place in Sioux Falls."

I turned to Bo and asked, "Where exactly we are going?"

"I've never been to the USGS before," Bo said as we headed down the hall. "I was hoping for a big door marked 'Shuttle Radar Topography Mission' or 'SRTM' or something like that."

We all glanced around. There were a few doors. But no signs.

"For a place that houses mapping data," Zack said with wonder, "they sure could use a map."

I laughed.

Jacob looked at his watch. "We're down to seventeen minutes before this cartridge runs out of time. We'd better hurry."

Just then, a door opened to our right and a woman

wearing a white lab coat over a long, flowered skirt entered the hallway. A group of kids about our own age were following her.

"The tour continues this way," she announced to the kids. "Next we will walk past a computer room where our scientists review satellite and Space Shuttle data."

"Space Shuttle data!" I cheered. "Let's follow."

We snuck in behind the group. We tried hard not to be noticed, but we were wearing old-fashioned U.S. Army uniforms that were too big and we were walking with a young Native-American woman with a baby strapped to her back. Kids in the class kept turning their heads to stare at us, and the woman leading the group began giving us suspicious looks.

We pretended not to notice their stares and walked along, heads held high, as if we belonged.

"So far, so good," Jacob leaned over and whispered in my ear. "But it won't be long before someone calls security."

"Hopefully before they do that, we'll find something that will convince Sacagawea," I whispered back, noticing that Sacagawea was playing with the beads on her dress again. Not interested at all in our surroundings.

The guide was wearing a name badge that said DR. LIZ BAKER. We followed Dr. Baker and the tour farther down the hall.

To our left, through a glass window, I saw rows and rows of computers on matching desks. Dr. Baker pointed at the computers and said, "This is a computer lab. Today, our data-gathering equipment is much more advanced than the tools Lewis and Clark had on their expedition." Suddenly interested, Sacagawea tilted her head to listen.

"In fact," Dr. Baker said, and looked directly at Sacagawea, "the United States Geological Survey was established in 1879 to continue the fine mapping and surveying work of Lewis and Clark."

Dr. Baker and Sacagawea locked eyes and held each other's gaze. They might have stayed there, staring into each other's eyes forever. But Pomp let out a mighty wail.

As hard as Sacagawea tried to quiet the baby, Pomp

just kept crying. We couldn't keep pretending we were part of the tour. We had to get out of there as quickly as possible.

I grabbed Sacagawea's hand and we all dashed into the computer lab. It wasn't private, but at least the baby wasn't shrieking in the hallway anymore. The door closed solidly behind us.

While Sacagawea bounced on her toes and sang a soothing chant, lulling Pomp to sleep, we watched as Dr. Baker led the tour farther down the hall, away from us.

"We totally lucked out," Bo said, looking around the empty room. "I don't know where the scientists are. But I'm sure that someone will be back soon. Let's show Sacagawea the SRTM data." He turned to Jacob and said, "If you can get a computer to work, I think I can explain to Sacagawea what the numbers mean."

Jacob sat at the closest desk and pressed a few buttons on a computer keyboard. "Uh-oh. I need a password to get into the system," he said, scratching his head. He pressed a few numbers. "Nothing." He tried a few more.

"We're running out of time." I begged Jacob to work faster.

"I'll help," Bo said. He went to stand next to Jacob, the two of them working together to crack the computer password code. While they were banging away at the computer keyboard, I explained to Sacagawea how, in our time, people rocket into space.

Zack told her all he knew about the Space Shuttle Endeavor and the SRTM mission to map the earth. Which wasn't much.

I always have a ton of questions, so when Sacagawea had a question about radar, my chest swelled with pride. The thing was, though, I didn't know how to answer.

"Do you know how radar works?" I asked Zack.

"Not even the smallest bit of an idea," Zack replied. "I try not to think about anything that has to do with cartography."

I nearly jumped out of my skin when a voice behind us said, "Radar is a signal that bounces off objects. It is then measured for strength and how much time the signal takes to return." I turned around to discover that it was Dr. Baker who'd spoken.

"Please don't kick us out," I begged. "We're only going to be here a few more minutes." I was panicked.

Before Dr. Baker could reply, Jacob shouted out, "I did it! I broke into the computer! You aren't going to believe it, but the password is the same as the one in that Internet computer game I was telling you about, LC Advent—"

"LC Adventures?" Dr. Baker interrupted. "I invented that game. Do you like LC Adventures?" she asked Jacob.

"I love it," Jacob replied, noticing Dr. Baker for the first time since she'd entered the computer lab. He was looking at her all moony-eyed, like she was a huge celebrity because she had invented a computer game he likes. "Are you going to call security?"

"And have us hauled off? Thrown out? Tossed in the street like garbage?" Zack added.

"No. I'm not going to throw you out," Dr. Baker said. Then she looked over at Sacagawea and asked, "Is that who I think it is?"

Since Sacagawea was still holding the translation stone, she understood Dr. Baker, pointed to herself, and said her own name. It was in Shoshone, but sounded close enough that Dr. Baker was convinced.

"Wow!" she exclaimed. Then she asked, "Where are you kids from, and how did you get Sacagawea here?"

"Well, we have this teacher . . . ," I started, then stopped. I had to make a split-second decision about how much to tell her. She was already a scientist, so I figured it wouldn't hurt. I quickly explained about Mr. C and the time-travel machine.

"Hmm." Dr. Baker pressed her lips together. "I've read articles about time travel, but had no idea that someone got a machine to work. Mr. Caruthers must be a really great inventor."

"But Mr. C has a problem." Jacob told her about Babs Magee and how we had to convince Sacagawea not to quit. "We think that if we can show her how the Lewis and Clark map will be important to the future, she'll want to help them." He also pointed out that we only had eleven minutes left to get the job done.

"Well then," Dr. Baker exclaimed, "let's get to work!"

She told us how scientists can make a topographical map by using the data collected by radar measurements. "Topography means the map shows the bumps on the earth, like mountains and valleys. It shows lakes and forests and cities. Plus, it pays attention to stuff that constantly changes, like volcanoes, earthquakes, and floods."

Sacagawea was really interested. Especially when Dr. Baker took over for Jacob on the computer and brought up some pictures. Even Zack leaned in to take a better look.

I paid attention too. And didn't even yawn one time. Dr. Baker was showing us some really cool stuff.

"These pictures aren't actually from the Space Shuttle data," she told us. "These pictures are from satellite images." Dr. Baker explained to Sacagawea about satellites in outer space, and what a photograph is.

"I want you to see the pictures from the Landsat 7 satellite," Dr. Baker said, pointing at the computer screen. "These are actual pictures of the Lewis and Clark Trail as seen from space."

She told us that by combining the Landsat 7 satellite pictures and the Space Shuttle data, the best maps of the earth's surface are being created.

Gathered around the computer screen, Dr. Baker showed us the Lewis and Clark Trail, focusing on the Camp Fortunate area. "On our maps, plants show up in shades of green. Rivers, lakes, and streams appear blue—"

"What about the ocean?" Sacagawea asked. I translated for Dr. Baker.

"Blue too," Dr. Baker went on, but I swear I saw that glint in Sacagawea's eye again. "Soil and rock formations are brown. Cities are purple." Dr. Baker was excited to show us all the parts of the map. She clearly loved her job.

Zack was studying Dr. Baker's map so carefully, I gave him a curious look. "Lewis and Clark never would have thought the Rocky Mountains were just a big hill if they'd had satellite and Space Shuttle maps!" Zack exclaimed at last.

Dr. Baker laughed and said, "They also thought that California was an island in the Pacific Ocean."

"It is not?" Sacagawea asked, quite seriously. That was an easy question. I knew the answer, but translated and let Dr. Baker reply.

"No," Dr. Baker replied, equally seriously. "It's definitely attached." She leaned forward to show the California coastline.

Jacob tapped the face of his watch, and we knew, no matter what Sacagawea had decided, it was time to go back to 1805. We told Sacagawea that we had to leave, but she kept staring at the computer images.

"So," she asked at last, "if we cross these mountains"—Sacagawea pointed at the screen—"will we find the ocean?"

I translated her question. "Yes," Dr. Baker confirmed. Sacagawea was looking at the Pacific Ocean.

"I want to see the ocean!" Sacagawea suddenly cheered so loudly, I was surprised she didn't wake up Pomp. "The water looks so beautiful from outer space." She reached behind her and patted Pomp on the head. "I cannot wait to see it up close."

"Guess what?" I told the boys. "Sacagawea finally has a dream!"

"Sacagawea wants to see the Pacific Ocean," Zack chimed over and over like song. He even made up a dance.

"Look who's singing and dancing now!" I exclaimed.

We were very happy, but Sacagawea wasn't finished dreaming. "I want to translate for Lewis and Clark. I want to travel over the mountains. I want to help them make their trades. I want—" She paused. And then, with a huge smile, she said, "I dream of helping Lewis and Clark map the west."

"We did it!" Bo said happily. "Now, instead of no dreams, Sacagawea has lots of them."

We thanked Dr. Baker. As we prepared to leave, Dr. Baker asked, "Can I see the time-travel computer?"

I didn't know if we should show her . . . she was a scientist, after all. She might want to come with us. Or she might decide to try to make her own time-travel computer. So before we showed her, Jacob made Dr.

Baker promise not to try to invent a time-travel machine. We already had a problem with Babs Magee.

Dr. Baker promised, and Jacob handed her our computer.

Dr. Baker took a quick look at it and gave the machine right back to Jacob. "It's amazing, but I don't want to time-travel," she declared. "I make maps!"

"And, of course, computer games," Jacob added, referring to LC Adventures.

"I wanted to make a game that teaches kids about the exciting adventures of Lewis and Clark," she told him. And then she said, "If you have trouble winning the game, try asking the Sacagawea character for help." She turned to Sacagawea and said, with a wink, "She always knows what to do."

Jacob smiled big and thanked Dr. Baker for the hint.

No one had come into the lab yet, so we decided to go ahead and leave from there. We only had nine minutes left and had to get Sacagawea back to 1805—and us back to school.

Jacob put in the computer cartridge, and the time-travel hole opened in the floor right beside Dr. Baker. She peered down through the green smoke and wished us luck on our journey.

Bo, Zack, and Jacob jumped in. I was going to go with Sacagawea, but before we left, Sacagawea turned around and said to Dr. Baker, "Your map will be the best map in your time. Lewis and Clark's map will be the best map in my time." I quickly translated.

Dr. Baker simply grinned. And without another word, Sacagawea and I blasted to the past.

9

Making Maps

Before I'd even steadied myself from landing, Sacagawea was off and running. We followed as best we could, but she was fast. Zack is the fastest runner in the whole third grade and even he was having trouble keeping up with her.

She went structure to structure, teepee to tent, looking for something. Or someone. Only when she found her husband did she finally stop. We were tired and my feet hurt.

"It's hard to run in moccasins," Zack said, wiggling his toes in the thin leather slippers. "I don't know how the Native Americans do it. If we ever come back here, we should bring extra tennis shoes. I bet we can trade one pair for four horses."

I laughed, imagining what Mr. C would say if we brought horses back to school.

Sacagawea was crouched low to the ground, speaking softly to Toussaint Charbonneau.

"Please, go tell Lewis and Clark that Chief Cameahwait is leaving Camp Fortunate," she said in a calm but urgent voice. "They must catch up to him and get his help with the map."

Charbonneau nodded, but didn't get up from where he sat in the shade of a willow. Sacagawea explained to him once more what she knew, but Charbonneau still didn't move.

"We're in trouble," I told the boys.

"It's worse than you think," Jacob said, studying the computer screen. "We only have six minutes." We decided to speed things up and go looking for Lewis and Clark.

"What's the deal with Charbonneau?" I asked Bo as we headed off.

"He was a good translator," Bo replied. "But he was really useless to the Corps. To be honest, Lewis and Clark didn't like him very much. Sacagawea did not choose to marry Charbonneau. The Hidatsa tribe sold her to him. Lewis and Clark wrote in their journals that he was lazy and mean to Sacagawea."

I imagined my own sixteen-year-old sister traveling with a husband she didn't know very well, a man whom Lewis and Clark disliked, and carrying a baby through the wild. She'd keel over and die the first day. Sacagawea was a true hero!

We quickly changed back to our own clothes, then found Lewis and Clark standing near the river.

I handed Captain Clark the pile of army uniforms and moccasins. He put them away, then said, "Chief Cameahwait instructed us to meet him here. He said he will draw a map in the sand showing us how to cross the great Rockies."

Captain Lewis looked so excited that he was about to finish this section of his map, I really, really wanted to break the bad news to him.

Bo shot me a look that meant I could NOT tell Lewis and Clark the chief was ditching them. "It's up to Sacagawea," Bo said just to me. "She has a dream now. Or two. Following one's dreams takes hard work. For Sacagawea, convincing Charbonneau is part of that hard work. We can't solve this problem for her."

I knew Bo was right, so I bit my tongue. Literally.

Willaim Clark was digging around in a nearby supply box. He had his journal in one hand, a compass in the other. He handed me the journal, Bo the compass, and went back to searching through the box.

He gave the two-pole chain to Zack. A triangle-shaped object with a telescope-looking top went to Jacob. William Clark explained that the tool was called a sextant and was used for judging our exact location.

They were ready for mapping. Only no one else had arrived. Not Chief Cameahwait. Not Sacagawea. Not Charbonneau.

Jacob looked at his watch. "Two minutes and counting," he warned. Over my shoulder, I saw a flash of yellow.

"Somewhere in those bushes," I told the boys, "Babs is spying on us."

"She still hopes Sacagawea will quit." Jacob shook his head, totally disgusted.

"Babs is wrong," Zack said, punching his hand in the air. "Way wrong." He pointed and said, "Because, look—Sacagawea's coming."

Sacagawea was running. The baby was bouncing on her back. Next to her was Charbonneau. He wasn't exactly sprinting, but he was walking fast enough. Sacagawea had brought François Labiche with them too.

In rapid-fire French, Charbonneau explained to Labiche, who then explained in English that the Shoshone chief was leaving. He was not going to help Lewis and Clark make the map.

Lewis asked Sacagawea what they should do.

Sacagawea turned to us and said quietly, "After all these years, I am happy I found my brother, but I am choosing to stay with Lewis and Clark and make the map. They really do need me."

She told the explorers, through the translators, that they must go to a mountain area where the

Native Americans were secretly gathering. If they hurried, they could stop Chief Cameahwait.

I almost laughed when Sacagawea told William Clark, "In the future, the USGS EROS Data Center will build on our map using SRTM and Landsat 7 imagery."

William Clark asked François Labiche to repeat the translation twice before he gave up trying to understand.

Lewis and Clark took the equipment from us before dashing off to find Chief Cameahwait. Charbonneau followed slowly behind, obviously in no hurry to keep up.

Before she left, Sacagawea turned to us and said, "Thank you. I now walk strongly with the spirit of the bear beside me." She smiled. "Let the animal spirits guide you as you continue on your many journeys through time." Then, she handed me her stone and went to stop her brother.

It was over. We had done our job and succeeded. Sacagawea now had a dream, many dreams, and it was time for us to go back to school. We knew history was back on track.

As we moved to a private place between two trees, Bo said, "Even with the directions the Shoshone will give them, it will take the Corps eleven days to cross the mountains. They will nearly die. Hunger will hit them so hard, they'll have to eat two of the Shoshone horses just to survive."

I wished the route across the mountains would be easier. But I knew that Sacagawea was so determined to help make the map and to see the ocean, nothing would stop their success.

Jacob pulled the cartridge out of the back of the computer. The time-travel hole opened, and we were ready to go.

"What's that?" Zack asked, looking off into the distance at another area between some trees. Green smoke was swirling over there. The same green smoke that was swirling on the ground near us.

"Babs!" Jacob, Bo, and I all said at the same time.

Our green hole was closing. We had to get back to school.

When we jumped back through time, we knew that Babs Magee was time-traveling too.

I swear, really swear, that as my feet left the ground and I began to fall through the hole, I heard a loud noise come from Babs Magee. I recognized the sound as the squeaking cry of an animal I'd only ever seen at the zoo.

It was the call of the weasel.

10

Excited

We landed near the creek behind our school.

"Whew," Zack said happily. "At least this time we didn't land in the water. My socks are still damp from 1805."

"Mine are too," I said, but I was so excited to tell Mr. C about our adventure, the soggy socks didn't really bug me too much.

We hurried over to join the rest of our class. Mr. C was collecting team journals.

"We had fun," Eliana Feinerman said as she handed him her group's book. She quickly showed the class how they'd drawn the map in the dirt, then carefully copied it into their journal.

Once Sacagawea caught up with her brother, this was exactly how Chief Cameahwait would make the map for Captain Lewis to copy.

I couldn't wait to hear more about their map in social studies class.

Shanika's group had made Eliana's map by correcting old maps from the library. I wondered how old mapmakers recorded facts about the creek. Were they right? Or way wrong, like the trapper maps that Lewis and Clark had to use and corrected? I was anxious to see Shanika's class presentation.

It was our turn to hand over our team journal. I knew our book was mostly blank. I started to sweat.

"Don't worry," Mr. C said with a wink. "I already have your team's journal." Pushing up his glasses, he asked, "How did it go?"

"In the end, we succeeded. But when we first got there—" I was about to tell him about Sacagawea's dreams, meeting Dr. Baker, and the sneaky dream-thief Babs Magee when Jacob gave me a shove and said, "TMI."

I stopped talking immediately. We'd have to tell Mr. C everything later, after the field trip. When we were all alone.

Mr. C was glad our special project went well. He gathered the class to return to school together.

We hung back while the other two groups rushed on ahead. "All right, Abigail," Mr. C said to me. "Now, I'd like to hear the details. What happened on your trip to 1805?"

I finally got to share TMI. I told Mr. C everything. Way more information than he needed. It felt good to tell it all.

When I finished, Mr. C sighed and said, "I'm worried about what Babs is doing. Maybe I should give up my new invention and time-travel myself instead. Now I finally understand why everyone on my list is quitting!" He smacked his thigh and exclaimed, "I can't believe she copied my list of famous people and stole Big Blue!"

"You can't quit too," I told him. "Someday we might be talking about what the world would be like if Mr. C never finished his new invention." As I said it, I wondered what he was working on.

"Please," Jacob begged. "We can handle this. We can convince all those people on your list not to quit."

"And someday," Zack added, "we'll catch Babs and get Big Blue back."

Mr. C was silent. He seemed to be thinking about whether we should still have History Club meetings. We were almost at school when he finally said, "All right, I won't cancel History Club. But you'd better watch out for Babs Magee. She's gone to the dark side, eh?"

"But the Force is with us," Zack said with a laugh.

"More than one force is protecting you kids," Mr. C said, glancing over his shoulder toward the trees.

I swear I saw something, or some things, moving out there by the creek. But this time, I wasn't scared.

At the back door to the school, Mr. C told us that History Club would meet again next Monday in the school cafeteria. He held the door open, but Zack blocked our way into the building.

"Mr. C," Zack said, "Jacob and I are supposed to walk home today, but I don't want to go yet. Can I use the office phone to call my mom and tell her I'll be late? I'm going to finish our team's map." Mr. C looked at him sideways. "Well, I mean, I'm going to start our team's map. And then I'll finish it."

"But your team doesn't have to make a map. Your team is going to report on Sacagawea," Mr. C reminded Zack.

"The other guys can tell about her," Zack responded. "I want to finish the map."

"It's not too B-O-R-I-N-G?" Mr. C asked Zack.

"No," Zack replied. "In fact, I love cartography!"

I nearly fell over, I was laughing so hard. Zack had found a new hobby. I hoped this one lasted longer than a week. "Well," I managed to say between giggles, "if Zack's staying, then so am I."

"As long as you're calling home, Zack, you might as well tell Mom I'm staying with you," Jacob told his brother.

"I can stay too," Bo said, asking if he could have the two-pole chain and compass. Bo would call his mom at work to let her know where he was.

Mr. C handed us back our equipment and team journal. He was thrilled that we'd decided to map the creek after all.

Being me, I had a few burning questions before we rushed off to do the project. "Mr. C," I asked, "would we catch up with Babs Magee if we left earlier?"

"It wouldn't make a difference." Mr. C shook his head and nibbled on his lip. "Big Blue is programmed according to Einstein's theory of relativity, which brings space and time together in a four-dimensional arrangement. On the other hand, your computer follows Sir Isaac Newton's conception of a three-dimensional space as having the property of motion, independent of the frame of reference in which it is measured."

I looked at him blankly. Jacob rolled his eyes. Zack yawned and said to me, "You had to ask, didn't you?" Only Bo looked interested. But Bo always looks interested.

Mr. C revved up to continue. "Because wormholes are a handle in the topology of space, therefore—"

"Stop!" we all shouted at the same time. Mr. Caruthers laughed.

"Mr. C," I asked, "are you trying to tell us that even if we left earlier, it wouldn't make a difference?"

"Exactly!" Mr. C cheered, as if he'd made it all crystal clear. "Now you understand why you can only time-travel on Mondays. Obviously, Babs must follow the order of my list, and no matter when you leave, she will always arrive first. It has to do with the subtle differences in the way the two computers were created and because of the space-time continuum. You see—"

I gave up trying to understand and I interrupted his thoughts with what I hoped was an easier kind of question. "Why does Babs always wear a yellow coat and matching hat?" I asked simply.

Mr. C came back to earth and answered. "Yellow was always Babs's favorite color. It's a bright color that gets noticed. And that's what she wants. You kids told me that her dream is to be famous. But we all know she's going about getting there the wrong way."

We left Mr. C muttering to himself about worm-holes and distortions of the space-time curvature.

Back at the creek, we were ready to map. We realized the first thing we needed to do was name the creek that ran behind our school. Just like Lewis and Clark had named Camp Fortunate after something good that had happened there, we wanted a name that reflected something good too.

The creek should be named after someone we admired. A true hero.

Zack opened our team journal, and there, on the first page, in big bold letters, he wrote: CARUTHERS'S CREEK. It was perfect.

Suddenly, I heard wild animal noises again: a growl. Scampering little feet. The chewing of crunchy leaves. A howl. And a loud, echoing roar.

"Did you hear it this time?" I excitedly asked the boys. They looked surprised because, this time, they definitely heard the sounds.

We all looked off into the shadows of the distant

trees. Our animal spirits were watching us: a rac-coon, an antelope, a coyote, and a mountain lion. They were guarding us. Protecting us.

And near them, we caught a final glimpse of Sacagawea's spirit, come to say good-bye. It was the spirit of the Dreamer. A large brown bear.

This is a copy of the map Captain William Clark created from the notes and drawings in his journal. Finished after the expedition in 1810, this map

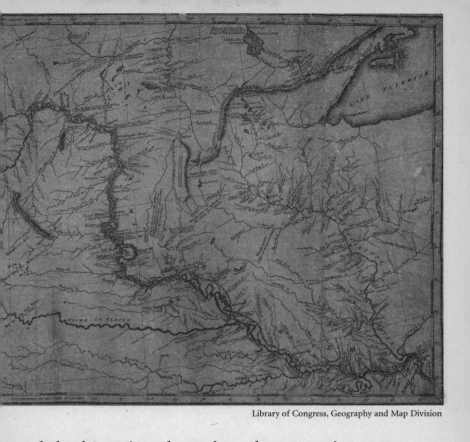

helped Americans learn about the new territory west of the Mississippi River.

The Golden Dollar coin was created to honor Sacagawea. The front of the coin shows Sacagawea and her baby, Jean-Baptiste. First created in 1999, the U.S. government has had trouble getting people to use dollar coins. Most of these coins are now in collections.

A Letter to Our Readers

Hi. We hope you enjoyed Sacagawea's Strength. Like the other Blast to the Past books, this story is a mixture of fact and fiction.

The fiction parts aren't true. Even though you might know kids like Jacob, Zack, Bo, and Abigail, we made them up. Your teacher may be super cool like Mr. C, but we made him up too.

The story of Sacagawea, though, that's a fact. Her life was recorded in journals by Captains Lewis and Clark and their exploration team, called the Corps of Discovery.

At age eleven, Sacagawea's tribe, the Shoshone, was raided by the Hidatsa Indians. The Hidatsa kidnapped many people from the tribe. She was taken with them, far from her homelands.

At sixteen, Sacagawea was married off to a French fur trapper she didn't know. His name was Toussaint Charbonneau. Lewis and Clark hired Charbonneau and Sacagawea to come along and work as translators. Two months after her baby, Jean Baptiste, was born, she strapped him to her back and went off with the Corps of Discovery to explore western America.

President Thomas Jefferson wanted the Corps of Discovery to find a river route across America from the Mississippi River to the Pacific Ocean. There was so little known about the area, he needed them to write down information about all the people, animals, and plants they saw. President Jefferson also wanted them to make a map of that new territory.

Just like in our story, Lewis and Clark used very old, incorrect maps and corrected them. Sometimes they had the Native Americans who lived in the area draw maps with sticks and stones in the dirt. Or, if the Native Americans had small maps written with charcoal on animal skins, Lewis and Clark would trade for them, collecting them whenever they could.

They also brought along equipment to make maps on their own, including a compass, a sextant, and a two-pole chain.

It would have been difficult, but Sacagawea might

have been able to quit and leave the expedition. When she discovered her brother was the Shoshone chief, many people wonder why she didn't stay with her tribe instead of going on with Lewis and Clark. We wondered that too.

Maybe making a map was her dream after all?

We'll never know. But what we do know is that Lewis and Clark would not have survived their journey without her. So, next time you look at a map, whether it's a street map of your neighborhood or an SRTM map of Earth's surface, take a second to remember Sacagawea's strength.

Have a blast,
Stacia and Rhody

P.S. Watch for Abigail, Jacob, Zack, and Bo's next Blast to the Past adventure when they meet Benjamin Franklin!

Here's a sneak peek at the sixth book in the
BLAST TO THE PAST series:

FRANKLIN'S FAME

Coming Fall 2006!

"Who do you think we'll meet today?" I leaned over
and whispered to Zack while Mr. C paused to
straighten his tie and run his fingers through his hair.

"Hmm," Zack wondered aloud. "Someone so
famous we can talk about him all week . . . maybe
Elvis Presley?" He played a little air guitar and wig-
gled his knee under the table. "Wouldn't it be rockin'
to visit The King?"

"Groovy," I said with a laugh.

Mr. C had cleaned himself up and was now pacing
in front of the room, lecturing as he walked.

"The man we will be learning about was an inventor, politician, soldier, statesman, poet, ambassador,
shop keeper, bookseller, printer." Mr. C stopped to
catch his breath, before adding, "Cartoonist, scientist, journalist, chess player, weight lifter, and loved
to read too."

Now I was certain it wasn't Elvis.

"Please get your textbooks," Mr. C instructed. "Turn to page one-forty-four. There, in the middle of the page, is a picture of an American legend: our famous forefather, Benjamin Franklin."

Mr. C started searching for the correct page in his teacher's guide, when Maxine Wilson's hand flew up in the air. "Excuse me, Mr. C," she interrupted. "There's no picture of Ben Franklin in my book."

Hands were popping up all over the classroom. Everyone was reporting the same thing: Ben Franklin was not in our textbooks.

Mr. C looked down at his teacher's guide. He had a confused look on his face. I could easily tell that Ben Franklin wasn't in there, either.

Khoi Nguyen raised his hand, and then reported, "There's a painting of some woman in the middle of page one-forty-four."

"That's odd," Mr. C said as he stood tall and slowly wandered toward Khoi's desk. "Just yesterday, I reviewed my notes for this morning's class." Mr. C scratched his head then pushed up his glasses. He glanced down at Khoi's book while saying, "I am certain that Ben Franklin is on page one-forty-four."

I looked at my own page 144. I checked the number. And then, double-checked.

It was true. Ben Franklin wasn't there. I quickly surveyed the painting of the woman. The small sketch was blurry.

Bo, Zack, and Jacob flipped though their books. We were all looking for Ben Franklin.

"Something isn't right," Bo said, rubbing his chin. The second thing I learned about him was that Bo always rubs his chin when he's thinking hard.

Turning to the index in the back of the book, Bo ran one finger down the names, then reported to us, "There's no Ben Franklin in our American history books at all."

I looked again at page 144. This time I only glanced briefly at the picture. I read the words under the drawing instead. I didn't even have to finish the whole page. When I realized the truth, I raised my hand so fast the motion shot me up and out of my chair.

"Be patient, Abigail," he said as he licked his finger and sped through the pages.

While I waited, I happened to look down at Bo. He was carefully reading page 144. His eyes went big like flying saucers when he also realized what was going on.

Jacob and Zack were still skimming through their own books searching for Ben Franklin.

"He's not in there," I told them, dropping my hand and coming around the table. I turned Zack's book back to page 144 and placed the textbook between them so they could view the page together.

"Stop looking at the picture. Just read the page, instead. It says right here," I pointed to the exact words: "'Babs Magee is the most famous statesman, inventor, and printer in American history!'"

Find out what happens in Fall 2006!